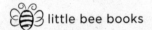 little bee books

An imprint of Bonnier Publishing USA
251 Park Avenue South, New York, NY 10010
Copyright © 2017 by Bonnier Publishing USA
All rights reserved, including the right of reproduction in whole or in part in any form. LITTLE BEE BOOKS is a trademark of Bonnier Publishing USA, and associated colophon is a trademark of Bonnier Publishing USA.

Library of Congress Cataloging-in-Publication Data is available upon request

Printed in the United States of America LB 0417
First Edition 10 9 8 7 6 5 4 3 2 1
ISBN 978-1-4998-0410-2 (hc)
ISBN 978-1-4998-0372-3 (pb)
littlebeebooks.com
bonnierpublishingusa.com

ELLA AND OWEN

KNIGHTS VS. DRAGONS

by
Jaden Kent

little bee books

illustrated by
Iryna Bodnaruk

TABLE OF CONTENTS

"If something in Terror Swamp tries to eat me, I'm totally blaming you," Owen said.

"Me?" his sister Ella replied.

1

"Yes, you!! Going to Terror Swamp was your idea, not mine."

"We can't disappoint Dad," Ella said. "He's expecting a stinky fish, and we're going to catch it for him." The fishing pole over her shoulder swung back and forth as her feet trampled through the forest.

The two dragons had left their home in Dragon Patch that morning with a promise to catch a stinky fish for their father. Unfortunately, as all dragons know, the best stinky fish swim in the muddy waters of Terror Swamp.

"Are you sure this is the way to our doom, I mean, Terror Swamp?" Owen asked.

"Don't you wanna see a real castle and a live knight?!" Ella asked.

"Why would I want to meet *anything* that wants to turn my beautiful scaly skin into a pair of dragon boots?!" Owen asked. "I don't want to be boots or shoes or sandals or—"

"Would it be better if they wanted to turn you into a hat?" Ella joked.

"There is *nothing* you can say to change my mind!" Owen huffed. "There's no way I'm going to that castle with you! No way!"

"Well, then I guess you'll just have to go back home by yourself," Ella said. "Back through the Fear Forest . . . the Field of Dread . . . and the Sands of Suffering . . . but you know best." Her wings fluttered. "Ta-ta, little brother." She flew off and headed toward the castle. Owen looked around, filled with fear.

"Okay, there's no way you're going to that castle *without* me!" Owen's wings fluttered faster and he took off after his sister.

The two dragons flew through the sky and into the clouds. In just a few minutes, the clouds disappeared, and before Ella and Owen was the castle of the knights who hate dragons.

The castle was made of stone blocks, with a high tower at each corner and a large wooden door.

Across the door was a big banner.

The two dragons landed behind a thick row of bushes near the castle. Owen pushed the branches apart and peeked out.

"Look at all the people in the village," Ella said. "They're singing. It's some kind of festival."

"Check out the banner over the castle door." Owen pointed. "This is our kind of party!"

The banner had only two handwritten words splattered on it: DRAGON DAY.

"I told you the knights weren't so bad," Ella said. "They celebrate dragons."

"Uh, Ella, what's that ugly thing under the banner?" Owen said.

There was a large bag of straw hanging from a rope. Four wooden sticks stuck out from the bag that looked a little like arms and legs. A pumpkin was tied to one end of the bag. Two eyes and a jagged mouth had been carved into it.

"I think that's supposed to be a dragon," Ella replied.

Four knights gathered around the "dragon." Villagers happily danced and stuffed themselves with meat and cheese and bread. An old bard with a long gray beard sat with his mandolin, but didn't play it. "Happy Dragon Day!" the crowd roared. "Happy Dragon Day!"

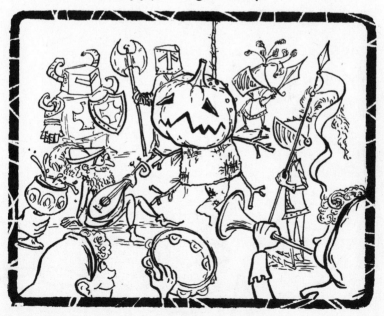

Owen smiled. "Maybe these humans aren't so bad after all if they have a *holiday* named after dragons!"

"Smash the dragon!" one of the knights shouted.

The villagers stopped dancing. They picked up tomatoes and apples from the festival tables and threw them at the bag of straw. The bard even used his mandolin to bash the fake dragon a few times.

"Happy Dragon Day," he sang.

"Wow," Ella said as they watched from their hiding place. "Worst holiday ever."

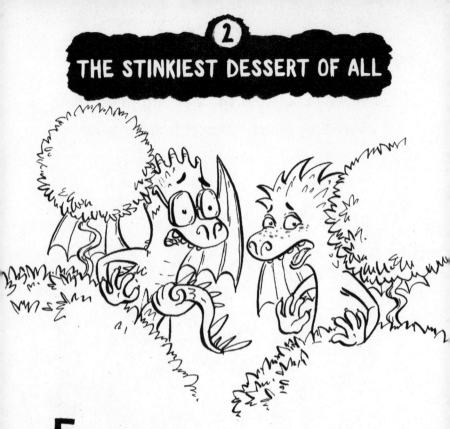

Ella and Owen backed away from the bushes, making sure not to step on a dry twig, rustle any noisy leaves, or trip over their own claws.

"We have to get out of here now," Ella whispered.

But Owen had stopped moving. He was sniff-sniff-sniffing the air.

Owen pointed toward the village feast. Leftovers were stacked on a table.

"Ella! Do you see what I see?!" Owen gasped. "A stinky fish strudel is on that table! It's the best dessert . . . ever!"

Ella shook her head. "I thought you said stinky fish *cake* is the best dessert ever."

"Pffft." Owen rolled his eyes. "Spoken like a dragon who's never had stinky fish strudel. I have a new plan that doesn't involve Terror Swamp." Owen pointed to the fish strudel on the table. "We can just get Dad that stinky fish strudel instead. We'll be heroes and nothing will eat me."

"I think your dragon brain has shriveled!" Ella replied. "That's a terrible idea."

"I know!" Owen said. "In fact, it's such a terrible idea, I'm surprised *you* didn't think it up!"

"Fine," Ella replied. "How do you plan to get your claws into that stinky fish strudel?"

"Easy," Owen said. "By using stealth-dragon tiptoe skills."

"We don't have stealth-dragon tiptoe skills," Ella pointed out.

"I do," Owen said. "I learned them from a book, *101 Ways to Be a Stealth Dragon*. Come on."

Owen tiptoed out of the bushes. He avoided stepping on a dry stick. He did not trip over a small rock. He dodged any prickly sticker cacti.

Ella followed close behind him.

Owen grabbed the stinky fish strudel
with his claws, but just as he was about
to leave, Ella tapped him on the shoulder.

"Trouble!" she whispered urgently.

The four dragon-smashing knights
stomped toward the table.

"HIDE!" Ella and Owen whispered,
looking at each other.

The twins scampered under the table.
The long tablecloth hid them from the
knights.

Owen listened as the knights ate the stinky fish strudel. He wanted to eat it and he wanted to eat it now!

"Can you smell it? It's—it's beautifully stinky!" Owen said. "So stinky beautiful. Stinky. Stinky . . . must have stinky fish strudel!" Owen's eyes were wide with hunger. But the knights were still eating! But the strudel! Could he grab it from the table without getting caught?

One of Owen's shaky hands crawled out from under the table. His claws slid over the table and grabbed a chunk of the stinky fish strudel.

"Yuck! What's with you and food that smells like moldy ogre socks?" Ella asked.

"All the best food smells like moldy ogre socks!" Owen replied. He held the fish strudel up to his open mouth.

Owen gobbled down the stinky fish in one bite and smiled happily.

Then Owen hiccuped.

Then he **BURPED** loud enough to rattle the table.

Ella slapped a hand over Owen's snout. "SHHHHH!" she whispered.

The four knights lifted the tablecloth and stared at the two dragons under their table.

"Behold!" said the first knight. "What's this under our table?"

"Uh . . . Happy Dragon Day?" Ella cracked a weak smile.

"**R**UN AWAY!" Owen shouted.

The table flipped over as Ella and Owen jumped out from underneath it. Food flew into the air. Cups spilled. Plates rattled. The knights jumped back, startled. Ella and Owen ran as fast as their clawed feet could carry them.

Ella huffed and puffed. "You know, we could *fly* away!"

"I-I can't!" Owen replied. "My wings are too scared to flutter!!"

The four knights took off after the dragons. "Get those things!" one shouted.

"Don't let 'em get away!" yelled another.

"Through here," Owen said, pointing at a pair of closed wooden doors of the castle. He crashed into them and bounced off. He tumbled to the ground and stopped in front of Ella.

"Castle doors are pretty strong," Ella said. She pulled the doors open. "And these are pull, not push."

Ella and Owen ran inside the castle. Owen shut the doors behind them.

CRASH! BANG! CLATTER-BA-BOOM!

The knights crashed into the closed doors from outside.

"Curse those running-away-from-us things!" said one knight.

"They have door magic!" said another.

Inside the castle, Ella and Owen scrambled across the courtyard. They ran passed a court jester who shook his rattle at them.

"Riddle me this: Why did the knight cross the road?" the jester asked.

"To get to the other side," Owen said as he and Ella rushed past him.

"To get to the—hey, how did you know that?" the jester exclaimed.

Ella and Owen ran into the nearest castle tower and up the stairs. "Castle towers always have places to hide," Owen said. "At least they do in books."

KLANG! KLANG! KLANG-KLANG! The footsteps of the knights *KLANG*ed on the stairs.

"They're coming!" Ella said. "Quick—in here!" She opened a door in the tower hallway and ran inside. Owen followed and closed the door behind them.

"Wow." Ella glanced around the room. "Owen, look where we are."

He turned and saw a room filled with swords, axes, spears, mallets, maces, poking sticks, lances, and a number of other pointy weapons that sent a chill up Owen's scales.

"Look over there!" Ella pointed to a row of knights' shiny armor. There were helmets, chest plates, and metal pieces for arms and legs.

"You're thinking of a really bad idea, aren't you?" Owen asked, even though he already knew the answer.

"A *great* idea, you mean," Ella said, smiling.

"Whatever it is, I'm against it," Owen replied.

"We can disguise ourselves as knights and sneak out of here!" Ella said.

"That idea's worse than my idea to get the stinky fish strudel, and *that* was the worst idea I ever had!" Owen said. He burped again. "Even if it was yummy!"

"These are perfect disguises. They'll never know it's us," Ella said.

"Never know?!" Owen cried out. "We're *dragons*! We have *tails*! And do you know what knights hate the most?! Tails! Because they're connected to dragons!"

"Do you have a better idea?" Ella asked.

"We could . . . or we could . . . but . . . then this could . . . or . . . ?"

"Any ideas at all, Owen," Ella said. She handed Owen a shiny metal helmet. "I dub thee Sir Worry-a-Lot."

"Ha-ha," Owen replied. He tried to squeeze his head into the helmet, but it was too small. He pulled and tugged and yanked until it POPPED into place. His snout stuck out from the visor.

Ella took a deep breath and wiggled into a piece of armor that wrapped around her body.

In just a few minutes, they were wearing full suits of armor and looked like large dragons stuffed into small cans.

"You're nuts!" Owen said as they looked at themselves in a mirror.

"Not 'nuts,' *knights*!" Ella said. "We're knights now!"

"You're nuts if you think the knights are nuts enough to think we're knights and not nuts!" Owen said.

"What?" Ella asked.

"I don't know. I didn't really understand it either," Owen confessed. "But you're *still* nuts and we're *not* knights!"

"Now here's the plan," Ella explained. "I'll open the door and we'll just walk out of the castle like we own the place and head to Terror Swamp. No one will know it's us."

Ella gently pushed opened the door. The four knights were standing in the hallway, looking right at them.

"What've we got here?" one of the knights asked.

"**W**hat are you doing in the armory?" said one of the knights.

"He is, I mean we is, I mean we are," Owen stammered.

Ella interrupted. "Hello, friends. This is the brave-knight-who-is-not-a-dragon, Sir Bonehead!"

"And this is Sir Stinky Feet!" Owen said and pointed to Ella. "We're from Not-Dragon-Land."

"It's, uh, very nice to, uh, meet humans like us who are not dragons!" Ella said. "We're just, uh, visiting your castle like knights-who-are-not-really-dragons do."

The four knights glared at Ella and Owen for a moment. Owen's dragon fangs began to chatter. Ella held her fire breath.

"I am Sir Dragon Crusher!" the first knight finally said.

"I am Sir Dragon Stomper!" the second knight proclaimed.

"I am Sir Dragon Thumper!" the third knight revealed.

"Let me guess," Ella said while pointing to the fourth knight, "you're Sir Dragon Masher-Basher-Crasher?"

"Uh, no. My name's Barry," the fourth knight replied. "Welcome to Camelnot!"

"Camel*not*?" Owen asked.

"Yeah! Originally, we were called Camel*lot*, but all the tourists were getting angry because there are no camels here," Dragon Crusher explained.

"So we changed the name to Nocamelot, but no one liked that. So then we tried Camelnotalot, and then Camel-less, Camelnada, Camelnone, Camelzero, No-camels-here-a-lot, Betty, Camelpalooza, and CamelCamel. And in the end, everyone voted for Camelnot."

"Well, that sure explains everything," Owen said.

"You'll love it here in Camelnot!" Dragon Crusher exclaimed. "We have all kinds of great festivals!"

"Like the Summer Festival of Brotherly Love," Dragon Stomper began. "Everyone in the castle gets together and bashes the straw out of a fake dragon!"

"And then there's the Spring Festival of Friendship," Dragon Thumper added. "People come to our castle from villages all across the land and we all smash the straw out of a fake dragon together!"

"But the *best* festival of all is the Winter Festival of Hugs and Kindness," Barry said.

"Ooooh! You're right! That *is* the best one!" Dragon Thumper agreed.

"Because you smack all the straw out of a fake dragon?" Ella asked.

"Don't be silly!" Barry said. "We all share in a great feast and show our kindness and love toward *all* creatures."

"That does sound kinda nice," Owen said.

"And *then* we smack all the straw out of a fake dragon!" Dragon Crusher said.

"Why do you hate dragons so much?" Ella asked.

"I don't know," Dragon Crusher said with a shrug. "Maybe because they're all made of straw?" he added.

"And if we ever, ever see a real dragon, we'll prove it's made of straw and hate it even more," Dragon Thumper said.

"We hate whatever they're made of!"
Dragon Stomper said.

"I hate dragons because my dad hated
dragons," Barry explained. "And my dad's
dad hated dragons, and *his* dad hated
dragons, and then his dad hated kittens,
but *his* dad hated dragons, and . . ."

"And his dad hated dragons. We get it,"
Ella said with a sigh.

"Actually, his mom hated dragons, but *her* dad hated dragons," Barry said. "Oh, and kittens, too."

"If none of you have ever even met a dragon, why do *you* hate them?" Owen asked.

"Because they're made of straw!" Dragon Crusher replied. "So, duh."

"No one told me there was going to be a test," Dragon Thumper whined.

POP!   POP-POP!

"What was that?" Ella whispered to her brother.

"Don't look now," Owen whispered back, "but your tail is about to pop out of your armor."

"Uh-oh," she exclaimed.

"Thanks, guys! It's been swell, but we gotta fly—I mean run!" Owen said in a panic. He grabbed Ella and pulled her toward the castle gates. "See you later, Dragon Crusher and Dragon Stomper and Dragon Thumper and Dragon Cupid and Dragon Donner and Dragon Blitzen!"

47

"Where ya going?" Dragon Thumper called out. "We were all gonna go see if there were any princesses locked up in towers by a mean witch and need saving!"

"Uh, we're going to Dragon Patch!" Owen said without thinking.

"Ooooh! We'll come along and help you knock the straw outta them dragons!" Dragon Stomper yelled with a cheer. "That's a lot more fun than saving princesses!"

An annoyed Ella shouted, "Dragons *aren't* made of straw!"

"Pffft. Then what *are* they made out of? *Dragon*?" Barry chuckled.

BOING! POP! SPRING!

Before Ella and Owen could make their escape, their knights' armor sprung off their bodies.

Snouts!

Wings!

Tails!

Claws!

Without any armor to hide their bodies, their true selves were revealed.

"Kittens!" Dragon Stomper shouted.

"Those aren't kittens! Those're, uh, um, uh . . ." Dragon Thumper scratched his head.

"Not kittens?" Ella asked.

"That's it! Not kittens! They must be DRAGONS!" Dragon Thumper shouted.

"RUN!" Owen shouted as he and Ella flew from the castle.

"CHASE!" Barry shouted and led the charge.

"We can't lead them back to Dragon Patch!" Owen said as the two dragons flew for their lives. "That'd be a worse idea than disguising ourselves as knights!"

"We need to lose them! What's the one thing knights hate more than anything?" Ella asked.

"Days!" Owen replied. "Get it? 'Cause they're *knights*?" Owen explained.

"Are your scales too scaly?!" Ella asked. "We're being chased by four knights with very long and very pointy swords and you're telling dumb jokes?!"

"Funny jokes!" Owen said.

"Dumb jokes!"

"Funny jokes!"

"DUMB JOKES!" Ella shouted.

The two dragons flapped their wings as quickly as they could, but they couldn't lose the four knights pursuing them on the ground below.

"I know! Let's fly into Terror Swamp!" Ella said.

"That idea is even worse than my last joke!" Owen said.

"It's a *great* idea! Even those knights aren't dumb enough to follow us into Terror Swamp!" Ella happily exclaimed.

WORST HOLIDAY EVER!

"Those sure are some dumb knights," Ella sighed and let out a puff of smoke as the knights followed them into Terror Swamp.

"Aw, dragon scales! What do we do now?" Owen asked.

Ella and Owen landed and were hiding behind a huge pile of moss that began to move.

"Uh, Ella? Why is our hiding place moving?" Owen asked.

"ROAR!" The moss-pile-that-was-not-a-moss-pile howled. Slimy moss arms covered in swamp beetles reached for Ella.

"It's a Beetle-Covered Bog *Moss*-ter!"
Owen shouted.

The green Beetle-Covered Bog Moss-
ter was covered in smelly moss and
towered above Ella and Owen. It looked
like a giant pile of cooked spinach with
legs, arms, and a huge mouth!

"GWAAAAAAAR!" the Beetle-Covered Bog Moss-ter roared as it chased Ella and Owen.

"There they are!" Dragon Crusher shouted the moment he spotted Ella and Owen.

"Dragon tails! Now we've gotta lose a Beetle-Covered Bog Moss-ter *and* four goofball knights!" Owen complained as they fled deeper into Terror Swamp.

"I've got an idea! Follow me!" Ella flew toward a distant light that was barely visible through the swamp vines and trees.

As they flew closer to the light, they realized it was a camp. A *troll* camp to be exact.

"I don't care if those trolls live in the most awesome tent in the world, we are *not* sneaking closer to get a better look," a worried Owen whispered.

"You don't need to tell me twice," Ella said with a gulp.

The two trolls in the camp were big. And ugly. And smelly. And very ugly. And hairy. And very, very ugly. And loud. And very, very, *very* ugly.

A banner that said HAPPY KNIGHTS DAY hung over the campsite. The trolls propped up a scarecrow dressed as a knight and cheered, "Hooray for Knights Day!"

"I'm really starting to think that we live in a very weird place," Owen said. "But what's the plan?"

As if to answer Owen, the Beetle-Covered Bog Moss-ter saw the trolls and fearfully ran in the opposite direction, leaving the dragons alone.

"See! *Everyone's* afraid of trolls!" Ella said.

"Including me!" Owen gulped.

"Now we just need the trolls to scare away those knights," Ella added. "Where are they, anyhow?"

Suddenly, the knights pounced on Ella and Owen, capturing them in a net.

"We got you kittens!" Dragon Thumper said with a chuckle.

"Dragons!" Barry corrected.

"Shhhh!" Dragon Stomper pointed to the HAPPY KNIGHTS DAY banner.

"Knights Day?" Barry read. "What's that?"

"Oh, just a little troll holiday." Ella pointed to the trolls, who kicked around the fake knight as if it were a soccer ball.

"Wow," Dragon Crusher said. "Worst holiday ever."

The sight of the trolls filled the four knights with dread.

"I bet those trolls would never be brave enough to do that to a *real* knight," Ella said, hoping to trick the knights into leaving her and Owen alone so they could escape.

"I know if *I* was a knight, I'd show those ol' trolls they couldn't mess with me," Owen said, with a sly wink to Ella.

The four knights looked at the huge trolls, who were at least twice their height.

"They sure are *big*. . . ." Barry said.

"And ugly . . ." Dragon Crusher said.

"If they're made of straw, we can crush them," Dragon Thumper quietly said in a timid voice. "You go first, Barry."

"I'm *always* going first! You go first, Dragon Crusher!" Barry said.

"I went first last time!" Dragon Crusher protested. "It's Dragon Stomper's turn!"

As the knights bickered about whose turn it was to go first because none of them were brave enough, Ella realized that the trolls had heard them and were coming this way.

"I think this would be a good time to hide!" she whispered to Owen.

The two dragons wriggled free from the net and hid behind a tree.

The four knights stopped bickering when a shadow fell over them. They looked up to see the big, smelly, and very ugly trolls looking down at them.

"What kind of kittens is you?" one troll asked.

"W-w-we're n-not k-kittens. . . ." Barry stammered. "W-w-we're k-k-k-k-k-knights."

"Them is the *worst* kinda kittens!" the second troll yelled with a huff.

"Mommy," Dragon Stomper squeaked.

The trolls snatched up the knights like little dolls and carried them back to their camp.

"Tails and snails! Now we can *finally* go home!" Owen started to fly toward Dragon Patch, but he was the only one in the air. "You know, we can't go home unless we actually *go home*," he said to Ella.

Ella didn't say a word. She just started to collect moss to make a disguise.

Owen slumped back to the ground. "Let me guess. You want us to save the knights from the trolls?"

"Yep," Ella said. "It's part of the Dragon Code."

"We don't have a Dragon Code," Owen replied.

"Well, we should have one," Ella explained. "And rescuing knights is a good way to start."

"Oh, fine!" Owen said, grabbing a handful of moss.

8

WORST PLAN EVER

"You did it, sis," Owen said as they flew toward the troll camp. "You actually came up with a plan a bazillion times worse than your last one."

Using the moss they had collected around Terror Swamp, the two dragons were disguised as troll fairies.

73

"We'll just tell the trolls that we're troll fairies and we're here to give them a wish," Ella explained. "And by the time the trolls figure out that we're not, we'll be long gone with the knights."

Ella fluttered into the troll camp. A frightened Owen followed, covering his eyes with his claws.

The four knights were tied to a tree next to the trolls, who were making a huge cauldron of lasagna.

"Oh, helllllllooooooo!" Ella chimed as she glided past one of the trolls. "My name is Sparkly Sparkle Glitter Pop! I'm a troll fairy and I've come to grant you a wish!"

"Me think us should eat it, Dumberdoor,"
one troll said the moment he saw Ella.

"Me think us should toss it into lasagna
and *then* eat it, Dumbdalf," Dumberdoor
answered with a grunt.

"B-but I'm a troll fairy! If you eat me, I
can't grant you a wish!" Ella cried with a
gulp.

"I, uh, thought troll fairies be smelly and ugly?" Dumbdalf asked.

"Have you met my brother, Smelly McUgly the troll fairy?" Ella nudged Owen forward.

"H-hi. I-I-I'm Smelly McUgly the t-t-troll fairy," a frightened Owen stammered.

"Wow, that one ugly and smelly troll fairy," Dumberdoor said in agreement.

"Now what would you like to wish for?" Ella waved her claws around as if conjuring magic.

"Um, me wish you get into lasagna so us eat you," Dumbdalf answered.

"Really? I can grant you a wish . . . *any* wish, and all you can come up with is to make me into lasagna?!" Ella was feeling more courageous. "Come on! I can grant you any wish you want! You guys've gotta think BIGGER!"

"Okay! Okay! Me got good one!" Dumberdoor said excitedly and smiled to Dumbdalf. "You ready? It totally best wish! Me wish that Sparkly Sparkle Glitter Pop *and* Smelly McUgly get into lasagna so us eat you both!"

"Ooooh! That *is* good wish!" Dumbdalf gave Dumberdoor a high five. "Me wish me thought of that one!"

"*Fine*. We'll both get into the lasagna so you can eat us," Ella proclaimed with a sigh. "But! Before we grant your wish, you must complete a challenge!"

"Is challenge to eat you?" Dumbdalf asked.

"No, you've gotta find . . . a talking platypus!" Ella said.

blah-blah blah-blah-blah

"A talking *pink* platypus!" Owen added to his sister's plan, hoping to make the task so impossible that the trolls would never be able to do it.

"Named Platyplat-plat-plat!" Ella said, trying to not giggle.

"And he has to play the ukulele!" Owen said, doing his best to not laugh.

"Upside down," Ella finished.

The two trolls scratched their heads, confused.

"Me gotta find talking pink what-a-pus named Platyplat-plat-plat. . . ." Dumberdoor began.

"And he gotta play uke-something, uh, upside down?" Dumbdalf added.

"You got it! Now get to it!" Ella cheered.

The none-too-bright trolls rushed off into Terror Swamp on their impossible mission.

"We'll never see those two again!" Ella excitedly flapped her wings faster.

"How come I've always gotta be the smelly and ugly one?!" Owen complained as he tore off his disguise.

"You know what they say: 'If the wings fit . . .'" Ella pulled off her disguise and used her claws to slash the ropes that held the knights.

"I . . . I don't understand. Why are you saving us?" a confused Barry asked.

"Because we want to show you that not all dragons are bad," Ella answered.

"Is *that* why we're doing this?!" A surprised Owen smacked the ground with his tail. "I thought we were doing this so they'd give us some stinky fish strudel!"

"And to get some stinky fish strudel," Ella added, wrinkling her snout.

"Thanks for helping us and showing us the error of our ways," Dragon Stomper said. "We'll never crush dragons again."

"There go all the best holidays," Dragon Crusher whined.

"Instead of using holidays as an excuse to attack fake dragons, why don't you use them as a time to really help others?" Owen asked.

"Oh yeah. That sounds *so much* more fun than bashing the straw out of dragons," Dragon Crusher said sarcastically.

"Is it too late to put them into the lasagna?" Owen asked Ella.

9
ALL'S WELL THAT ENDS WITH NO ONE GETTING EATEN

Ella, Owen, and the four knights returned to the castle and were greeted with cheers of "Hurray! Hurray! The knights of Camelnot have captured whatever those things are!" by the villagers.

"No! No! No! We didn't capture them!"
Dragon Crusher quickly corrected.
"They're our friends!"

"They're dragons," Dragon Thumper
explained.

This shocking news was met by a chorus of cheers. "Hurray! Hurray! The knights of Camelnot made friends with evil dragons!"

"No! No! No! They're nice!" Dragon Stomper quickly corrected. "Not all dragons are evil!"

"Not evil?!" a villager named Byron said with a scoff. "Next you're gonna try to tell us that they're not made of straw!"

"We're not!" Ella finally spoke up.

"Then what are you made of?!" Byron laughed. "*Dragon?!*"

"It doesn't matter what they're made of," Dragon Stomper added. "What does matter is that we've been wrong about them this whole time and we need to treat them as equals!"

"*Equals?!*" a villager named Gwendolyn gasped. "There go all the best holidays!"

The bard held up his mandolin. "What am I supposed to do with this if I can't bash straw dragons with it?"

"You could try playing *music* with it," Owen said.

"You can play *music* on these things?!" the shocked bard asked. "*Really?*"

"And now, to give thanks for all that Ella and Owen have done for us, we knights of Camelnot have taken new names!" Barry announced.

"From henceforth, I shall be called Sir Dragon Buddy!" Dragon Crusher called out.

"And *I* want to be known as Sir Dragon Pal," Dragon Stomper proclaimed with a cheer.

"And *I* will be Sir Dragon Don't-Quite-Love-Them-Yet-But-Don't-Exactly-Hate-Them-Anymore," Dragon Thumper said.

Barry proclaimed, "And from this day forward, I shall be forever known as . . . Carl."

The knights and villagers of Camelnot bowed deeply as Ella and Owen waved good-bye—but not before Owen made sure to get the stinkiest fish strudel in the castle.

"I'm waiting. . . ." Ella said as they flew down the path.

"You're right, sis," Owen said. "This was all *your* fault."

"I meant that I'm waiting for you to admit that my plans are better than yours," Ella replied.

"Nope," Owen said.

"Yep," Ella replied.

"Nopey-nope-nope-nope-nope."

"Yeppy-yep-yep-yep-yep."

THUD! THUD! THUD!

The two trolls from Terror Swamp suddenly rushed out of the forest toward them. Ella and Owen skidded to a stop in midair.

"We got 'um! We got 'um!" Dumbdalf shouted. "Hey! What happened to all your moss?"

"We, uh, wished it away!" Ella explained, as they no longer had their troll fairy disguises.

Owen was the first to realize this could only mean more trouble for him. And probably Ella, too. The two dim-witted trolls had somehow found a platypus. A *pink* platypus carrying a ukulele to be exact, which he played . . . upside down. Somehow.

Owen gulped. "Oh, no. Please don't tell me your name is—"

The pink platypus cut off Owen and sang, *"You got it. My name is Platyplat-plat-plat and I love to siiiiiiiing!"*

"Me did what you said!" Dumberdoor said with a snarl. "Now me want us wishes!"

"And me wish you get in the lasagna!" Dumbdalf added, thrusting the cauldron of lasagna before Ella and Owen.

Ella and Owen exchanged a worried look.

"Got any more bright ideas?" Owen whispered to Ella.

Unfortunately, Ella didn't have any ideas at all this time!

Read on for a sneak peek from the fourth book in the Ella and Owen series, *The Evil Pumpkin Pie Fight!*

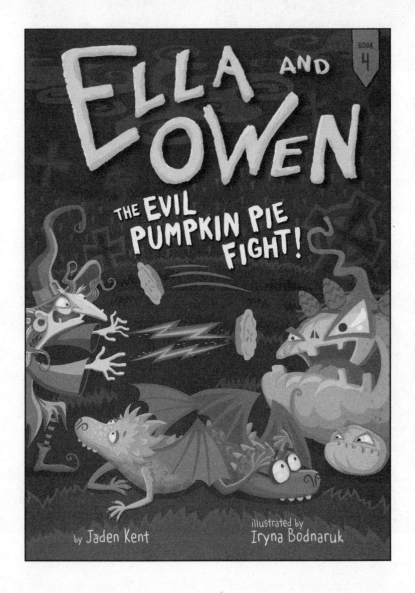

ELLA AND OWEN

BOOK 4

THE EVIL PUMPKIN PIE FIGHT!

by Jaden Kent

illustrated by Iryna Bodnaruk

A HEAD FOR TROUBLE

"**G**ive us me wishes!" Dumberdoor the troll said.

"We found the pink platypus that plays the ukulele upside down!" Dumbdalf, the other troll, said. "Now you owe us wishes."

The two trolls raced from the forest toward Ella and Owen. The two dragons were shocked. "How did they find a pink platypus?" Owen asked his twin sister.

"I don't even want to know about the ukulele," she replied.

"So, where's me wishes?" Dumberdoor demanded.

"Okay, okay. I have your first wish," Owen said. The trolls rubbed their hairy, wart-covered hands together with excitement.

"Your first wish is that you wish you could watch me and Ella run away!" Owen and Ella turned and ran away.

"Me not want that wish!" Dumberdoor said. "Me wish for dragon stew!"

"Me too wish for stew dragon!" Dumbdalf added. "Grant me wish!"

The trolls watched as the two dragons ran into the forest and disappeared into the shadows.

"I think we lost them," Ella said.

"I hope so," Owen puffed. "My claws are aching from all that running and my wings are too tired to flutter."

Owen looked around. "Wait a minute! We're back in Terror Swamp again! I didn't want that either!"

"Don't worry. I think home is this way," Ella said, pointing through the forest, ". . . or maybe it's that way."

"Good," Owen replied. "You go that way. I'm going the other way." Owen ran away, but crashed into a tree. A branch broke off and fell on his head. "It's a Swamp Tree Goblin! It's got me!" Owen's scaly body wobbled and he tripped over a tree stump. He crashed into Ella.

"Watch where you're going!" she cried.

Ella and Owen splashed down into the inky black doom of Terror Swamp.

Ella shivered, shaking the water from her scales. "Don't be such a scaredy-dragon," she said. "There's hardly any water here."

Owen stood up and picked the mud off of his claws. "Great. So we're lost again."

"Maybe not," she replied. Ella pointed toward something moving on the other side of some trees. There was a flickering light in the distance. "Let's check that out," she said.

"Oh, let's not," Owen replied. "Every time we go to check out something, we get captured and something tries to eat us."

"It could be a way out of Terror Swamp," she said.

"Really?!" Owen said. "There's no way I'm going to investigate the only light glowing in the middle of a place called Terror Swamp!" Owen folded his scaly arms. He wasn't budging.

"Well, I'm going to go see what it is. You can stay here. On your own. In the dark." Ella's dragon wings fluttered and she flew off toward the light.

Owen looked around as it grew darker. Leaves rustled and swirled in the night air. A Grizzly Owl hooted. A Swamp Bat swooped low, passing by Owen's snout.

On second thought, being left all alone while someone else goes to check out the only light glowing in the middle of a place called Terror

Swamp is even worse than going to check out the only light glowing in the middle of a place called Terror Swamp! Owen thought.

Owen flew off after his sister. "Okay, Ella! Wait up! Let's see what's making that light!"

Together the two dragons pushed through the forest. They came to a clearing in front of a broken-down wooden swamp shack. A jack-o'-lantern with an angry face carved into it sat on the porch. Light flickered from the candle inside its head.

"That's one creepy jack-o'-lantern!" Ella said.

"Okay, we've seen what the light is. Let's leave," Owen said. "This place looks haunted."

"You can't ever go," the jack-o'-lantern suddenly said to them. "Ever-never!"

"Who-who are you?" Ella stuttered.

"I am . . . the Pumpkin King!" he said. "Vines up!"

"Ahhhhhhhh!" Ella and Owen screamed.

Vines stretched out from beneath the porch and wrapped around Ella and Owen.

"I told you something like this would happen!" Owen yelled.